For F.L.W., a great dad who always made me
look up words in the dictionary.
Thanks for all the free rides up the stairs!
- S.R.

In loving memory of my dad
and to my husband, Craig, for the new memories
we're building together.
- L.W.

I Love My Daddy
© 1995 by Scharlotte Rich
Illustrations © 1995 by Linda Weller

Requests for information should be addressed to:

Zonder**kidz** ™

The Children's Group of ZondervanPublishingHouse
Grand Rapids, Michigan 49530
www.zonderkidz.com

Zonderkidz is a trademark of The Zondervan Corporation
ISBN: 0-310-70104-X

I Love My Daddy was previously published by Gold-N-Honey, a division of Multnomah Publishers.

Printed in Singapore

00 01 02 03 04 05 /HK/ 10 9 8 7 6 5 4 3 2 1

Scharlotte Rich

I Love My Daddy!

ILLUSTRATIONS BY LINDA WELLER

Zonder**kidz**

The Children's Group of ZondervanPublishingHouse

Introduction

Fathers come in lots of different shapes, sizes, and colors.

They live in many different
kinds of places.

They have many different
types of jobs.

$\mathcal{B}$ut one thing is always the same.
They have a *very* special place in their
hearts for their children.

I have a really special daddy.
In the morning, Daddy and I talk
while he shaves. Sometimes he says,
"Here, Buddy! You need a shave!"

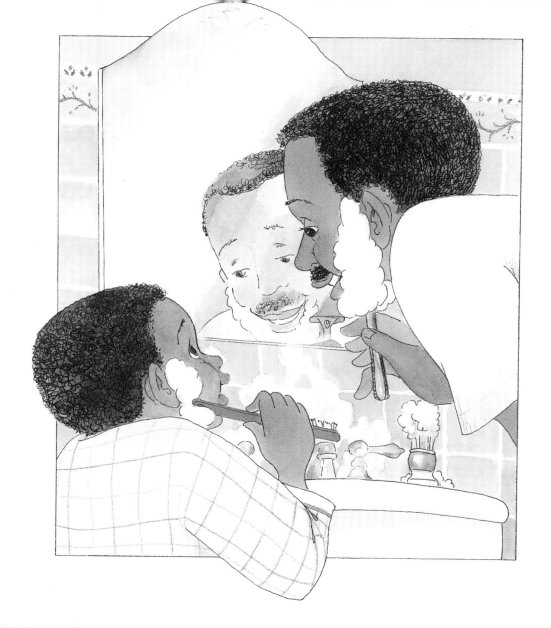

We are alike in many ways.
Our hair is the same color.
And people say I have my daddy's smile.
I like to walk like Daddy, too.

Some mornings we go out exploring.
One morning Daddy said, "It's fall, Tiger.
Let's go appling!"

We got in the car and drove a long way.
We sang songs about Jesus.
Daddy can sing really loud!
"Daddy! Look at all the cows and sheep!"

"The Bible says we're like sheep,"
Daddy said, "and Jesus is our Shepherd.
He takes good care of us."

Daddy turned on a dirt road and stopped.
"This is the place!" he said.
We jumped out next to a big red barn.
There were cats playing in the yard.

$\mathcal{I}$ saw lots of green trees
in long rows that stretched out forever.
Daddy called it an orchard.

Apples were everywhere!
Red apples. Green apples. Yellow apples.
There were big jugs of apple juice
and bunches of vegetables, too.

I helped Daddy pick out apples.
They had long, funny names like Jonagold and
Pippin. Daddy knew all the different kinds.
Then we bought a box of honey made
by the farmer's bees.

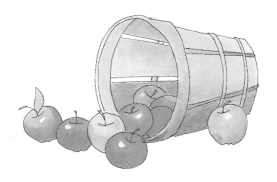

"Hello there," said the farmer.
"Would you like to see something special?"
Daddy put me on his shoulders,
and we followed the farmer.

$\mathcal{I}$ climbed a fence and looked over.
A cow was looking right back at me!
"Bessie is one of my best milk cows,"
said the farmer. "She likes to have
her ears scratched."

The farmer took us inside
a chicken coop. There were noisy
chickens everywhere!
I helped him fill the feeders with grain.

When we got home,
we stored the apples in the garage.
Daddy made up a silly song about apples,
and we sang while we worked.
I had a special day with Daddy.
I love my daddy and my daddy loves me.
That's just the way God planned it to be.

A Snowy Day with Daddy

When I woke up this morning,
I saw ice on my window.
It was silver and sparkled in the sunshine.
Daddy called it frost.
"God makes beautiful things, doesn't He?"
said Daddy.

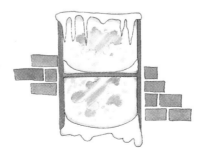

"Daddy! Look at all the snow!
Can we go sledding? Please?"
"Today is Saturday," Daddy said,
"and I don't go to work. But we need to
do a few chores around the house.
Then we'll go sledding."

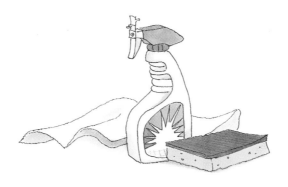

$\mathcal{F}$inally, after lunch, Daddy swung me
around and said, "Let's go play in the snow!"
We put on so many warm clothes
I could hardly move.

"What do you want to do first?"
Daddy asked.
"Let's make snow angels," I said.

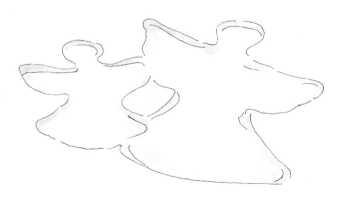

Next we built a giant snowman.
I put one of Daddy's old caps on his head.
I named the snowman George.

$\mathcal{T}$hen Daddy
took me for a really fast ride on the sled.
Cold wet snow flew all over my face.
"Faster, Daddy, faster!" I shouted.
We went down the hill about twenty
times until Daddy said,
"Peanut, I think it's time to go home;
let's take our last ride.

It was getting dark.
I asked Daddy why God didn't make
the sun stay out all the time.
Daddy said, "God made a time for everything.
There's a time to work, a time to play,
and a time to rest."

When Daddy tucked me in that night,
he said God made the darkness so people and
animals could sleep and rest for
the next day.

"Daddy, you know about everything!
When I grow up I want to be just like you!"
"Goodnight, Peanut," Daddy said. "I love you."

I love my daddy and my daddy loves me.
That's the way God planned it to be.

Camping Out

One day Daddy and I decided to camp out in the back yard.
We searched around in the garage until we found the tent and the sleeping bags.

We spread out the tent on the ground.
There were lots of pegs.
Pound, pound, pound! Daddy and I hammered
the pegs into the dirt.

$\mathcal{T}$hen we got long sticks
and poked them up inside the tent.

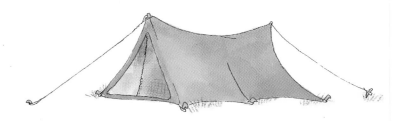

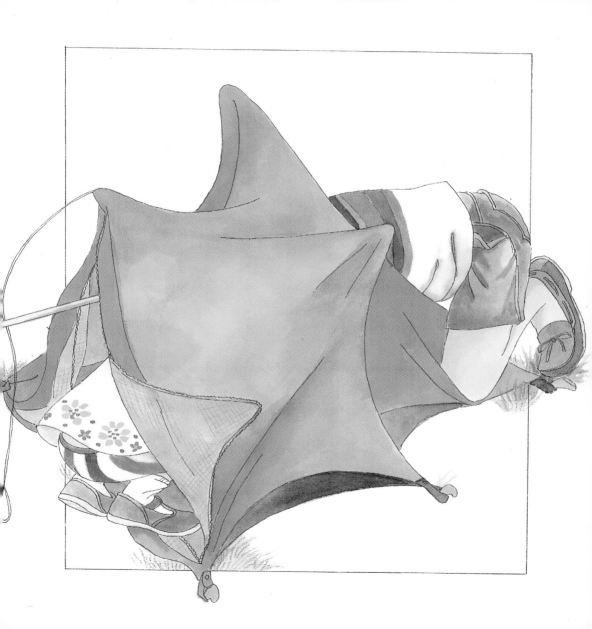

We went into the kitchen and
packed some food.
I brought my lion for protection.
I said, "He can help guard the tent."

"You know," Daddy said,
"Jesus is called a lion in the Bible.
He's with us everywhere we go, so we don't
have to be afraid of the dark."

Daddy built a fire and cooked dinner.
When it was dark, I looked at the stars.
There were so many we couldn't count them.
"God made all the stars," Daddy said,
"and He knows the name of each one.

$\mathcal{D}$addy and I said our prayers.
Then I got sleepy and snuggled down into
my sleeping bag.

"Goodnight, Little Camper,"
Daddy said. "I love you very much."
I love my daddy and my daddy loves me.
That's the way God meant it to be.

At Home with Daddy

Sometimes Daddy
and I play ball in the back yard.
We're good ballplayers.

"Time to go in and get ready for bed,
Sleepyhead!
Stand on my shoes and I'll give you a
free ride up the stairs."

$\mathcal{I}$ get ready for bed and then we have a wrestle–and–tickle time. Daddy and I do lots of circus tricks, too.

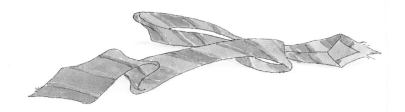

We always have a story time.
Daddy uses lots of funny voices when he reads.
Sometimes he makes up silly stories
right out of his head.

$\mathcal{I}$ have a special
Bible book we always read last.
Daddy says the Bible is the most special
book in the whole world.

When Daddy turns off the lights,
we pray and talk together.
I can ask any questions I want.
Tonight I asked, "Daddy, do you love me?"

"Yes. You are my child and I love
you very much."

"But Daddy, will you always love me?
No matter what?"
"Yes, I will always love you, no matter what.
And I love you more and more
every day."

"But Daddy,
do you love me even when I get into
trouble and do bad things?"
"Yes. Even when I'm angry with you,
I still love you."

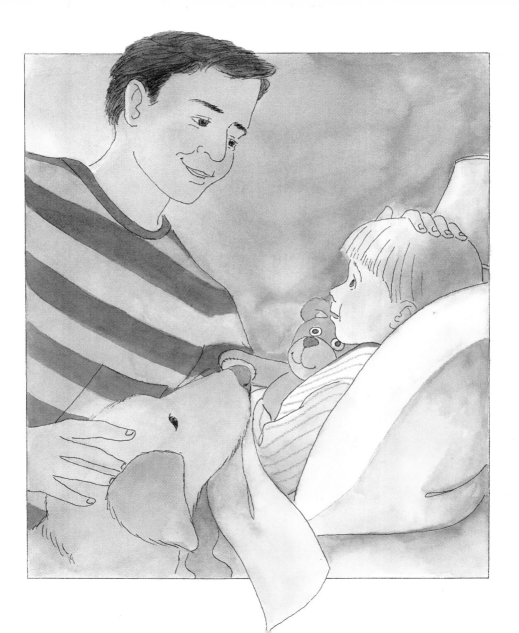

"But Daddy, why do you love me?"
"Well, I love you for lots of reasons, Squirt.
I love you just because you are you.

"You are a special gift from God and I prayed
for you even before you were born."

"Listen to this and always remember it:
I love you more than there are stars in the sky.
I love you more than all the sand by the sea.
I will always love you, no matter what!
Now close your eyes, Hugbug,
and go to sleep!"

I really love my daddy and
my daddy loves me. That's the way God
planned it to be.